Max's Glasses

by Vin Dacquino
illustrated by Karen Leon

TABLE OF CONTENTS

CHAPTER 1

The Broken Recorder

Max Freeman could see a little bit—but not much. "I wish I could *really* see," he said, "like other kids."

Max's mother put her hand on his shoulder. "I know you do, Max," she said sadly.

Max's mom was a small woman with curly brown hair. She was a scientist, but it was Sunday, so she wasn't at the lab.

"How are your new glasses working out?" she asked.

Max pushed them up on his nose. "No other kid in third grade would be seen wearing glasses as thick as these," he said. "And they don't even work."

"Well, homework time, I guess," his mother said, mussing his hair and giving him a kiss on top of his head.

The new tape recorder Max's teacher had lent him was on the table by his bed. He stuck his pillow behind his head and pressed "Play."

"*Hello, Max. Are you ready for your homework?*"

Max hated Mrs. Crowley's voice. He could tell she didn't like making homework tapes for him. She just had to do it because he couldn't see well enough to read his homework assignments.

"*Today we are going to learn about inventions, Max. This tape recorder is an invention. I bet you didn't think of that.*"

"This is *so boring*," Max thought.

Then he grabbed his pillow and threw it. The recorder fell to the floor with a crash.

"Max?" His mother shouted from downstairs. "What was that noise?"

"I just—uh—dropped something," he said.

He gathered the pieces quickly. "Oh, man!"

He grabbed his phone and pressed quick-dial memory button number one to call his best friend, Tommy. If anyone could put the recorder back together, it was Tommy Ping.

"Please answer," he whispered softly.

"Hello?"

"Tommy, you gotta help me. I just killed Mrs. Crowley," said Max.

"WHAT?" Tommy shouted. "Max, you killed Mrs. Crowley? Really?"

"Not exactly," said Max, "but I broke her new tape recorder."

"Oh," said Tommy. "That's bad, but we can probably fix it. Now if you'd really killed Mrs. Crowley . . ."

"OK, OK," said Max. "Just get out your tools and glue."

CHAPTER 2

The House at Bangor and Main

"Max, where are you going? Did you finish your homework already?" Max's mother called as Max ran out the door.

"Uh—almost," he said. "Tommy is going to help me with just one little thing."

"Don't stay too long," his mother warned him. "Homework comes first, remember?"

"C'mon, Shadow," Max called to his black Labrador retriever. "We're going to Tommy's."

If anyone knew how to get to Tommy's, it was Shadow. But at the end of the driveway, Shadow pulled Max to the left instead of going right.

"Hey!" Max said. "That's the wrong way!"

Shadow ignored him. He practically dragged Max down Main Street to an old abandoned house on the corner of Bangor and Main. Shadow stopped and sat down in front of a red door on the side of the house.

Without warning, the door creaked open. A tall figure came out and stood before them. Max struggled to focus. Was it a man or a woman? Then the figure spoke, and Max knew it was a man. In a deep voice, the man said, "Hello, Max."

CHAPTER 3

Tommy Ping, Boy Genius

"Where've you been?" Tommy asked from his front porch. "I've been waiting out here for ages."

Max didn't talk.

"Hey," Tommy said, "are you OK? Why is your face so white?"

"Something strange just happened," Max said. "Shadow dragged me to the old house on Bangor and Main."

"The haunted house?" Tommy asked.

"Yeah, that one," said Max. "And this real tall guy came out of the house."

"So?" said Tommy. "What's the big deal about that?"

"He knew my name," said Max. "And I know I never saw him before."

"Weird," Tommy said. "Maybe he is someone you know, but you just couldn't see him that well."

"No way," said Max. "I would have recognized him because he was so tall— I mean really, really tall. And I always recognize voices. I know I never heard this guy's voice."

"Weird," Tommy repeated. Then he pointed to the bag in Max's hand. "Is that the recorder?"

Max lifted the broken tape recorder. "Yeah. This is it."

Tommy took the bag and dumped the contents on the porch. "This isn't so bad. The doors to the battery compartment just came unsnapped. We don't even need glue."

In a minute he had the recorder back together again.

"C'mon," he said. "We're going to Bangor and Main. I've got to see what's going on there."

Max frowned. "I don't think we should go there."

Tommy ignored him. He led Max to the garage and grabbed a flashlight. Then he ran into the kitchen and started putting some apples and cookies into a paper bag.

"What are you doing?" asked Max. "Why are you taking all that stuff?"

"We're taking a flashlight so we can look around without turning on any lights. And we're taking food so if we get trapped in the house, at least we won't starve to death."

Now Max really didn't want to go back to the house on Bangor and Main. Sneaking around in the dark and maybe getting trapped in the house with some big weird guy who knew his name didn't sound like his idea of fun.

"Come on," said Tommy. "We've got to get to the bottom of this."

Max respected Tommy for being a boy genius, junior inventor, private detective, and tape-recorder repairman. So he went along.

CHAPTER 4

In the Workshop

As Max, Tommy, and Shadow got near the house, Shadow started acting strange again. He lifted his head and howled.

"Wow!" Tommy said. "This is so cool!"

"Yeah, really cool," Max said nervously.

"Is that the door?" Tommy asked, pointing to the red door the man had come out of.

"That's it," said Max, "but I really don't think . . ."

Tommy walked up to the door before Max could stop him, then ran back. "What happened?" Max asked.

"The door is open!" Tommy said.

Tommy grabbed the front of Max's shirt. "Let's go in."

"I can't see anything," Max said. "Can you?"

Tommy pulled out his flashlight and shone the light ahead of them. They moved along slowly, and Tommy let out another loud "Wow!"

"Shhh," Max said. "He'll hear us."

"Max?" Tommy said. "Can you see any of this? There are gadgets all over the place. This is some kind of workshop— an inventor's or a scientist's."

Tommy went from gadget to gizmo. He was fascinated by the levers, buttons, and colored flashing lights. He carefully touched a red button, and everything went dark.

"I think I blew a fuse," Tommy said.

"I turned off the power," a deep voice said. Max stood frozen at the familiar voice and the shadow of the huge man.

"We didn't mean to disturb you," Tommy said, nervously. "We just stopped by to, uh, bring you some lunch." He dropped the bag of food and the boys darted out the door with Shadow close at their heels.

CHAPTER 5

A Secret From the Past

"We need to go back there later, Max. Did you see all the neat stuff he had in there?"

"Are you crazy?" Max asked.

"Max? Tommy? Are you two out there?" Max's mother shouted. "Tommy, why don't you stay for lunch?"

"Thanks, Mrs. Freeman," Tommy said. "But I have to be home by noon."

"It's almost noon now. You'd better hurry," she said.

"See you later," Tommy said, and hurried away.

Max's mother set out a large bowl of soup just as Shadow let out another howl.

"Why is he acting so strange? I've never seen him do that."

"Uh—I'm not sure," Max said.

"Maybe you should take him for another walk after lunch. Have you finished listening to Mrs. Crowley?"

Max felt sick. He had left the tape recorder at the strange house.

"Are you all right, Max?" his mother asked. "You look pale."

"Mom?" he asked, changing the subject, "Did anybody live in that old house on Bangor and Main when you were growing up?"

"It's funny you should ask," she said. "My favorite teacher lived in that house. His name was Roger Pierce. He taught science, and he was an inventor."

Max's mouth dropped open.

"In October, right about this time of year, Mr. Pierce disappeared. No one ever found out what happened to him." She sighed. "I still wonder." Then she added proudly, "He was really a genius—and I was his star pupil."

Shadow started howling louder than he had ever howled before.

"Max, you'd better take Shadow for that walk. He sounds awful."

CHAPTER 6

Max's Choice

Shadow nearly knocked Max over. "We're going back there," Max told Shadow. "I've got to get that tape recorder back."

Shadow barked and led the way to the old house.

Max took a deep breath and knocked on the red door.

"Come in, Max," said the deep voice as the tall man opened the door.

Max jumped back, frightened. "How do you know me?" he asked.

"I know quite a bit about you, Max. Your mother was my most brilliant student."

Max couldn't speak. When he found his voice again, he asked, "Are you Mr. Pierce?"

"Yes I am, and you have nothing to be afraid of, Max," said Roger Pierce. "I was hoping to see your mother during my short visit, but I'm almost out of time. I tried to reach her through my thought transmitter," he continued, "but I got your dog instead. It's hard to send thought transmissions back in time."

"What are you talking about?" Max asked. "There's no such thing as a thought transmitter."

"There is where I come from, Max," said Roger Pierce. "Many years ago, on a day very much like this one, I took a trip—a trip into the future."

Max just stared. He was speechless.

"For years I'd been working on a machine that would let people travel in time," Mr. Pierce explained. "Then one day it actually worked. The trouble is, I couldn't get back. So I made a whole new life for myself in what you would call the future. That's my time now."

"How come you're back here now?" asked Max, not knowing whether to believe Mr. Pierce or not.

"In the future I still live in this same house," Mr. Pierce explained. "And I still work on my machine. Yesterday I did something that brought me back to your time, but I don't know exactly what I did. I know how to get to the future again, but I'm not sure I can ever get back to your time again. So this may be my only visit."

"What's the future like?" Max asked, still not sure if Mr. Pierce was telling the truth.

"It is an amazing place," answered Mr. Pierce. "There are new things that you can't imagine. We do use thought transmitters to send one another messages. And Max, you wouldn't even need those glasses. We cured eye problems years ago."

"Can I go there with you?" Max asked. "Will you take me with you so I can see like everyone else?"

"I could, Max, but I couldn't make any promises about getting you back home. Are you willing to give up your parents and friends?" He bent over and patted Shadow's head. "And Shadow?" he asked. "If you want to join me, I'll take you. But I have to get back very soon, so you have to decide now."

Max thought of his parents. He thought about Tommy. And he thought about Shadow. He even thought about Mrs. Crowley, who spent all that time making those tapes for him. She really wasn't so bad, after all. How could he just leave all the people he cared about? When you really thought about it, his life was pretty good, in spite of those glasses.

"I've made my decision, Mr. Pierce," Max said. "Thank you anyway."

"I understand," Roger Pierce said. "And I have some good news for you. Right now, doctors and scientists are working to help people see better. Just have patience, and one of their inventions will help you one day. Believe me, I know."

Then Mr. Pierce reached out and handed Max his tape recorder.

"Tell your mother I'm very proud of her," he said.

Then he walked over to the machine Tommy had been fooling around with earlier. He pushed a button, pulled a lever…and disappeared.